Opuestos en la escuela / Opposites at School

Fuerte y suave en la clase de música

Loud and Quiet in Music Class

Eileen Greer

traducido por / translated by Rossana Zúñiga

ilustrado por / illustrated by
Joel Gennari

PowerKiDS press.

New York

Published in 2018 by The Rosen Publishing Group, Inc.
29 East 21st Street, New York, NY 10010

First Edition

Translator: Rossana Zúñiga
Editorial Director, Spanish: Nathalie Beullens-Maoui
Editor, English: Melissa Raé Shofner
Art Director: Michael Flynn
Book Design: Raúl Rodriguez
Illustrator: Joel Gennari

Cataloging-in-Publication Data

Names: Greer, Eileen, author.
Title: Loud and quiet in music class = Fuerte y suave en la clase de música / Eileen Greer.
Description: PowerKids Press : New York, [2018] | Series: Opposites at school = Opuestos en la escuela | In English and Spanish. Includes index.
Identifiers: LCCN 2017013186| ISBN 9781508163497 (library bound book)
Subjects: LCSH: English language–Synonyms and antonyms–Juvenile literature.
  | Music–Instruction and study–Juvenile literature. | Language arts
  (Primary) | Language arts–Correlation with content subjects. |
  Interdisciplinary approach in education.
Classification: LCC PE1591 .G718 2018 | DDC 428/.1–dc23
LC record available at https://lccn.loc.gov/2017013186

Manufactured in the United States of America

CPSIA Compliance Information: Batch #BW18PK. For further information contact Rosen Publishing, New York, New York at 1-800-237-9932.

Contenido

Contents

Estoy muy emocionada. ¡Hoy es mi clase de música! Mi maestro es el señor Sandler.

I'm so excited for music class today! My teacher is Mr. Sandler.

¡Hacemos muchísimo ruido!

We get to make tons of noise!

6

Me gusta tocar la batería.

I like playing the drums.

¡La batería suena fuerte!

The drums are loud!

El señor Sandler dice que la música puede ser fuerte o suave.

Mr. Sandler says music can be loud or quiet.

9

El señor Sandler nos enseña
a cantar suavemente.

Mr. Sandler teaches us
to sing quietly.

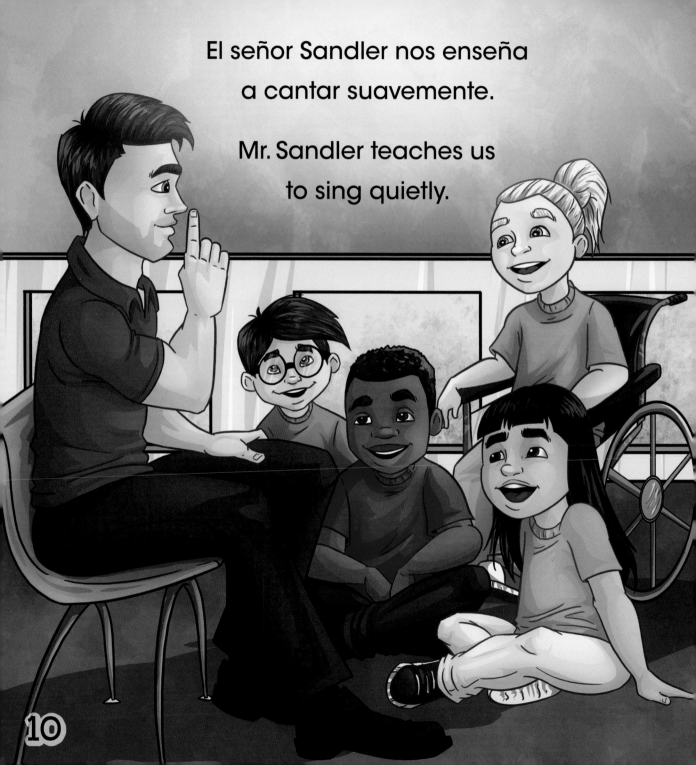

Después, lo hacemos más fuerte.

Then we get louder.

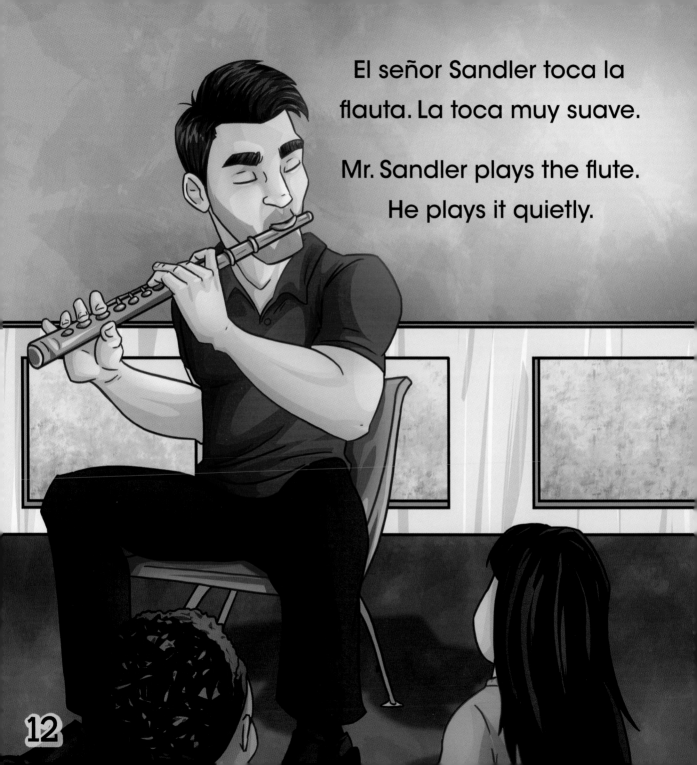

El señor Sandler toca la flauta. La toca muy suave.

Mr. Sandler plays the flute. He plays it quietly.

12

También toca
la tuba.

He also plays
the tuba.

14

La tuba puede sonar muy fuerte.

The tuba can be very loud.

Intento el triángulo. Si lo golpeo recio, suena fuerte. Si lo hago suavemente, suena suave.

I try the triangle. If I hit it hard, it's loud. If I hit it softly, it's quiet.

17

Todos tratamos de tocar los instrumentos.

We all try playing instruments.

¡Sonamos muy fuerte!

It's getting pretty loud
in here!

19

El señor Sandler aplaude tres veces.

Mr. Sandler claps his hands three times.

Eso significa que guardemos silencio.

That means be quiet.

Terminó la clase de música. ¡Fue divertido hacer música fuerte y suave!

Music class is over. It was fun being loud and quiet!

Palabras que debes aprender
Words to Know

(la) batería
drums

(la) flauta
flute

(la) tuba
tuba

Índice / Index